P9-DNW-413

WITHDRAWN
Anne Arundel Co. Library

ART & MAX

To Dinah!

Clarion Books
215 Park Avenue South, New York, New York 10003

The illustrations were executed in acrylic, pastel, watercolor, and India ink.
The text was set in Century Schoolbook and Magma Halo Italic. Book design by Carol Goldenberg

Clarion Books is an imprint of Houghton Mifflin Harcourt Publishing Company.
www.hmhco.com

Library of Congress Cataloging-in-Publication Data
Wiesner, David. Art and Max / David Wiesner. p. cm.
Summary: Max wants to be an artist like his friend Arthur, but his first attempt at using a paintbrush sends them on a whirlwind trip through various media, with unexpected consequences.
ISBN 978-0-618-75663-6 [1. Artists—Fiction. 2. Artists' materials—Fiction. 3. Painting—Fiction. 4. Lizards—Fiction.]
I. Title. PZ7.W6367Art 2010 [E]—dc22 2010005205

Printed in Malaysia
TWP 10 9 8 7 6 5 4
4500771625

ART & MAX

DAVID WIESNER

CLARION BOOKS • HOUGHTON MIFFLIN HARCOURT
Boston New York 2010

Careful, Max!

Hey, Art, that's great!

The name is Arthur.

I can paint too, Arthur!

You, Max? Don’t be ridiculous.

Oh, all right.
Just don't get in the way.

Arthur?
What should I paint?

Well…you could paint me.

You? Really?

What are you doing?

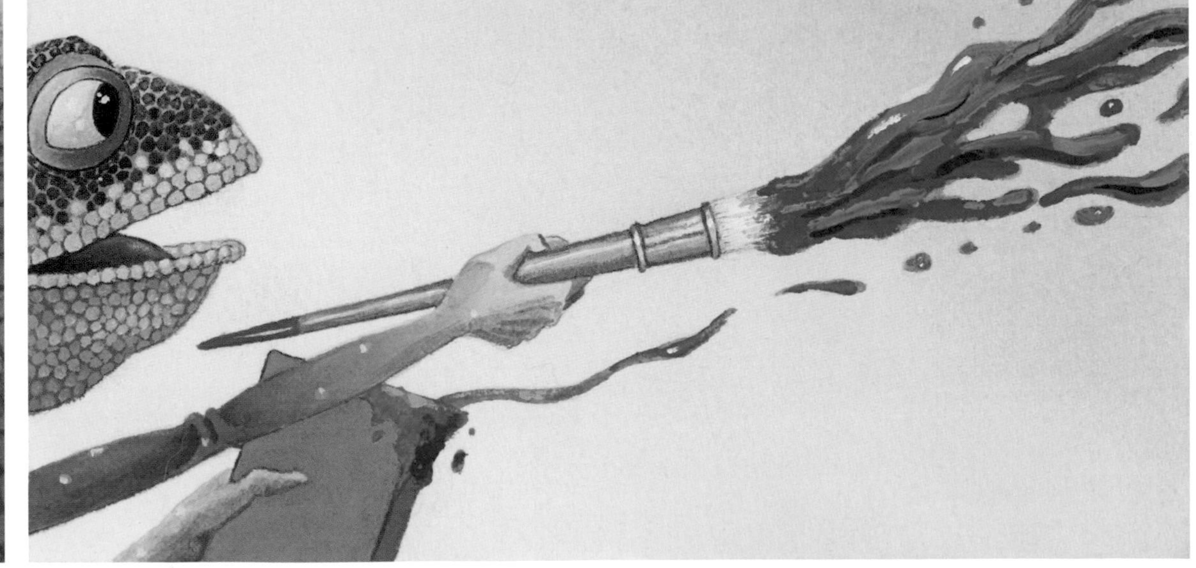

I'm painting you!

Ta-da! What do you think?

This is preposterous!

Ooh! Turn around—

I missed a spot.

MAAAAX!

Wow!
Oh, Max…

…what have you done?

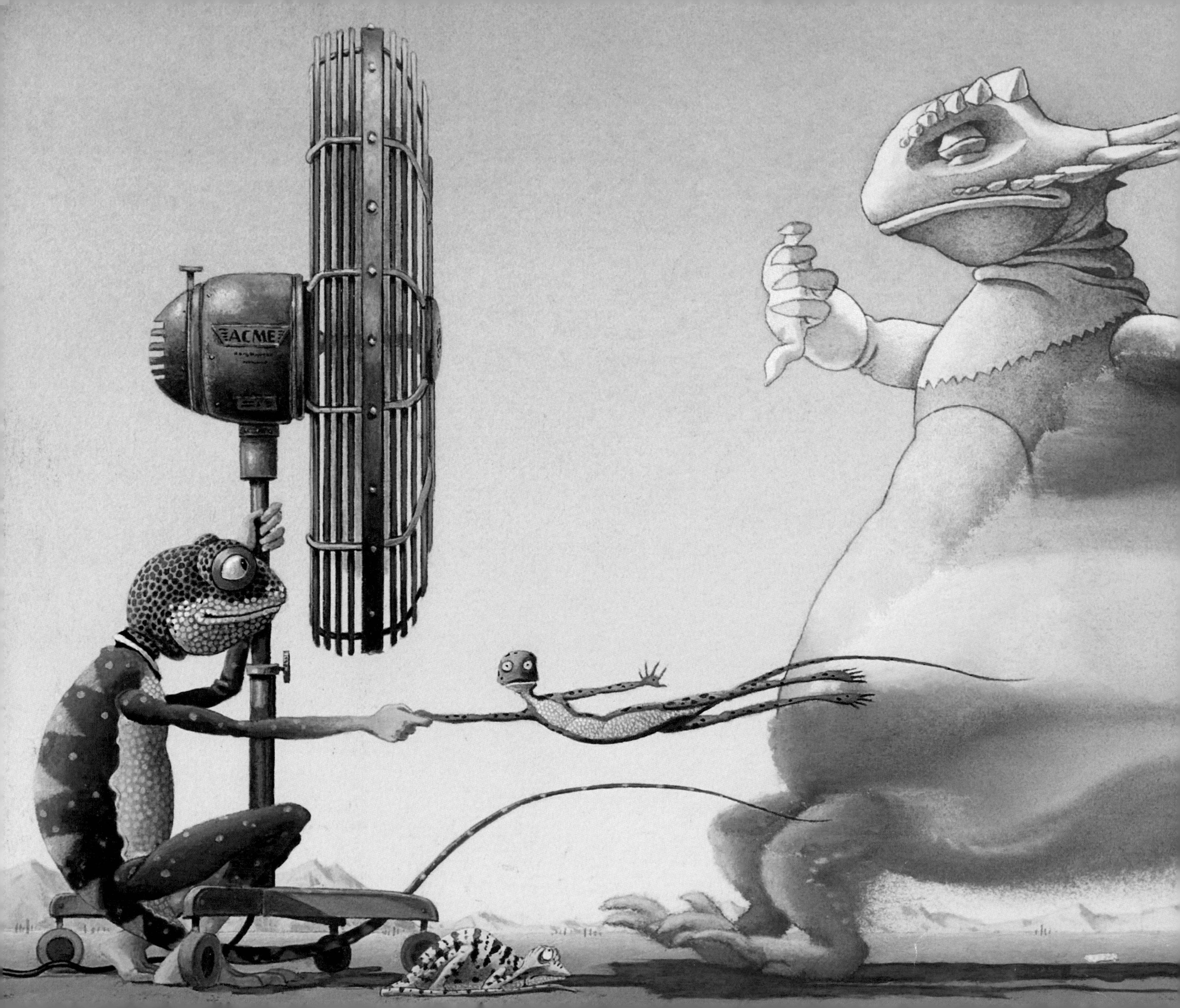
ACME

I feel…strange.

Have a drink of water.

I'll get some more!

Oooohhh!

Hold on, Art—

It's *Arthur!*

Don't go…

Arthur?

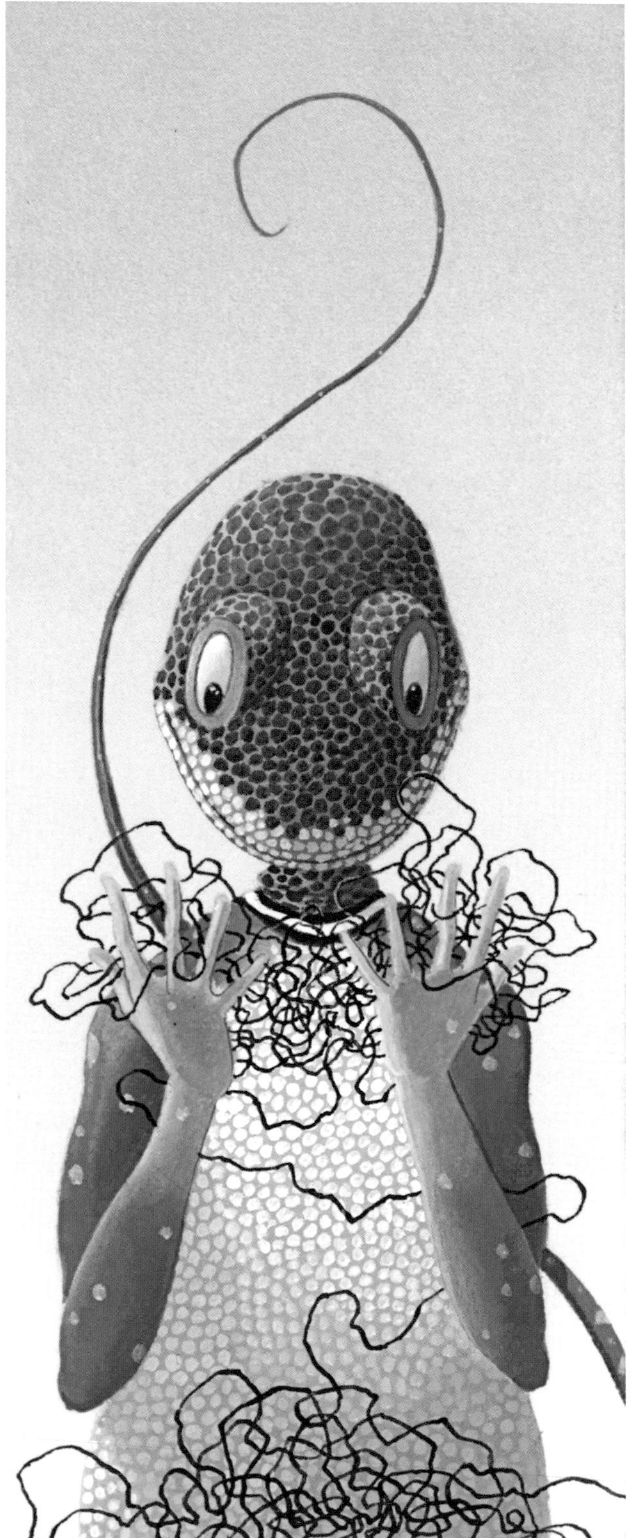

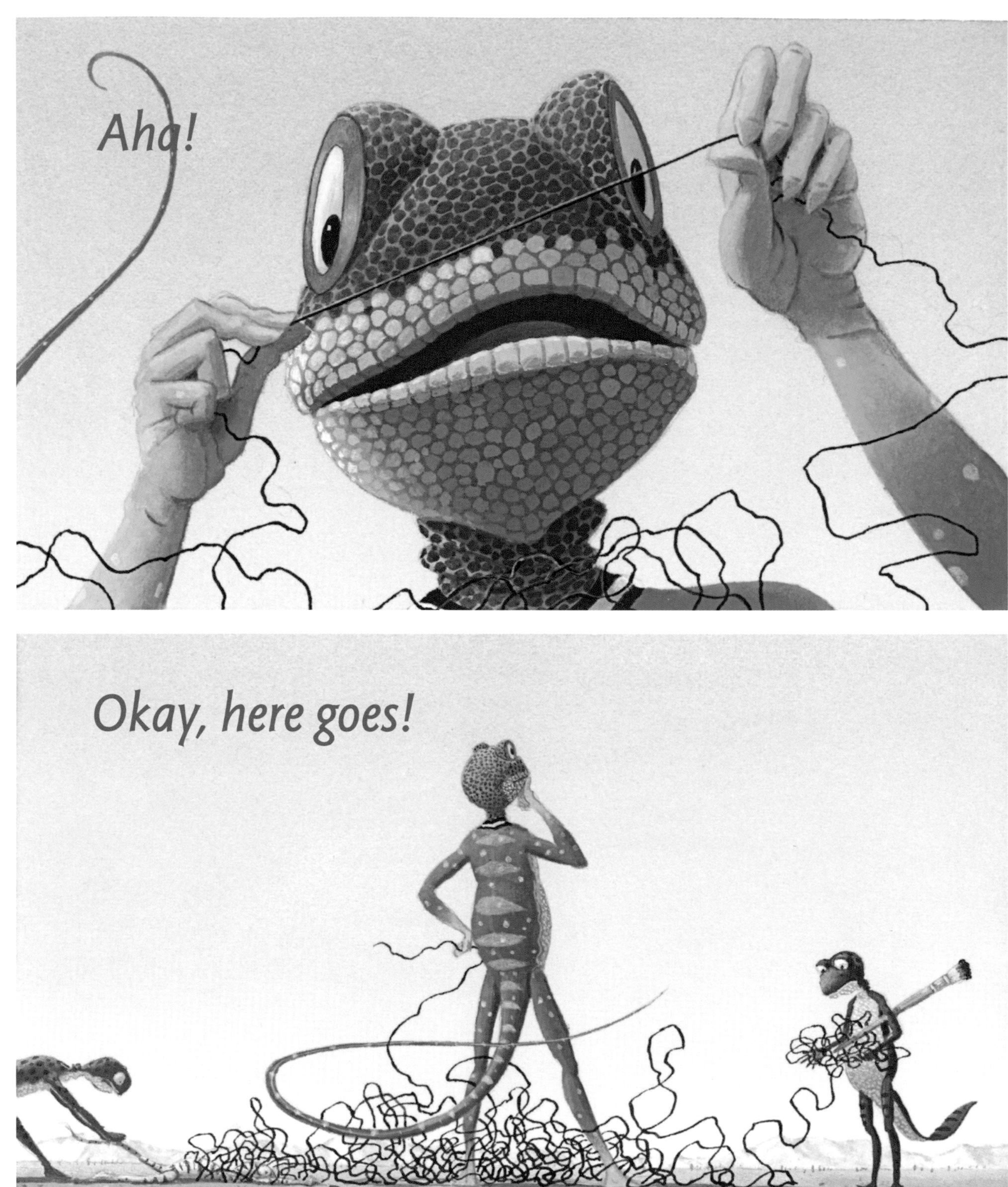
Aha!
Okay, here goes!

More detail, I think.

Yes, pointy bits like this…

How's that?

Acceptable, I suppose.
But don't forget my foot.

Come back here!
You're not finished!
ACME

Now what?

Just hold still, Arthur!

ACME

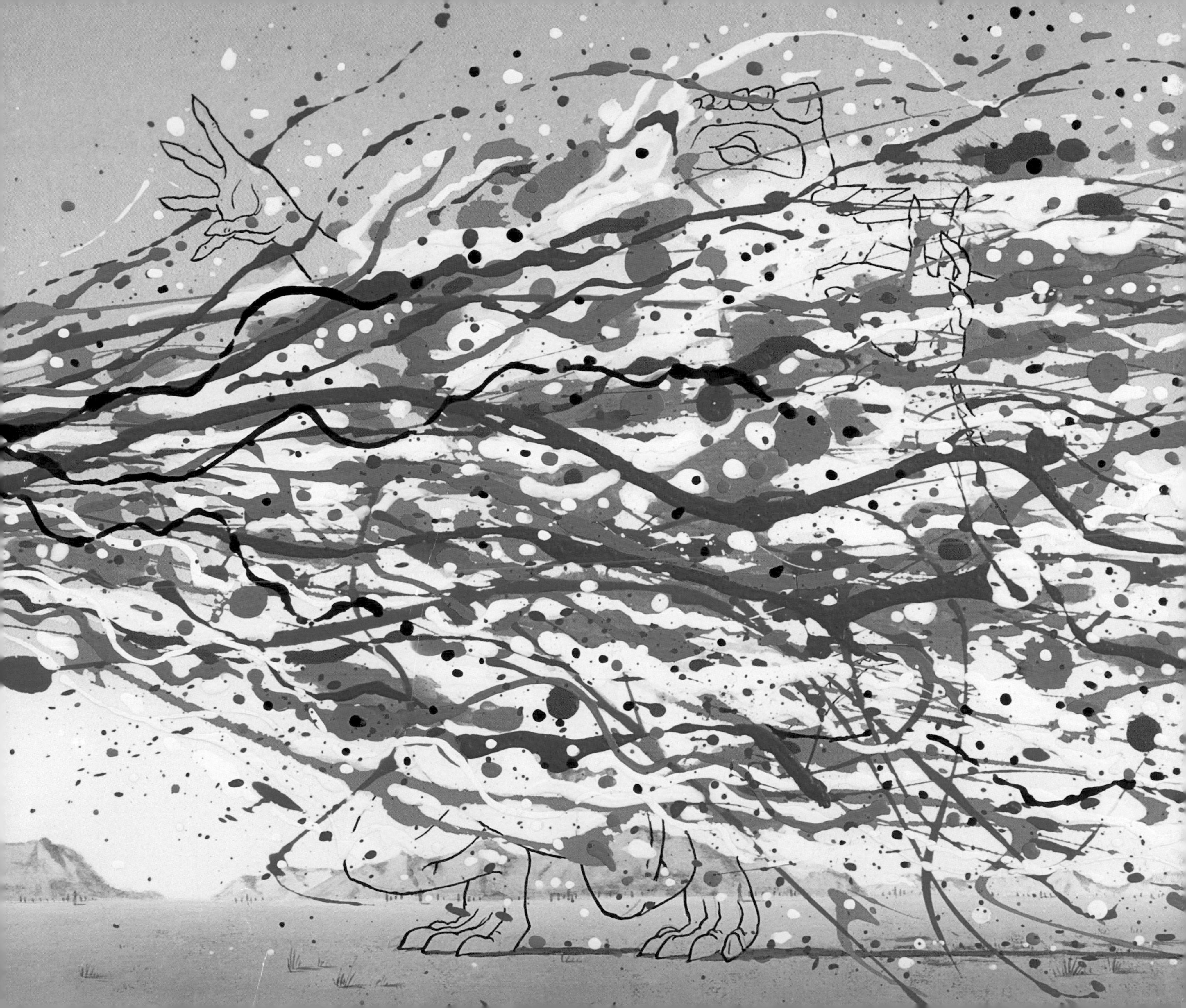

Fascinating.

Yes! Yay!

Let's paint some more!
All right, Max,
let's get started.